American edition published in 2019 by Andersen Press USA,
an imprint of Andersen Press Ltd.
www.andersenpressusa.com

First published in Great Britain in 2019 by Andersen Press Ltd.,
20 Vauxhall Bridge Road, London SW1V 2SA.

Distributed in the United States and Canada by
Lerner Publishing Group, Inc.
241 First Avenue North
Minneapolis, MN 55401 USA
For reading levels and more information, look up this title at www.lernerbooks.com.

Color separated in Switzerland by Photolitho AG, Zürich.
Printed and bound in Malaysia.

Library of Congress Cataloging-in-Publication Data Available
ISBN: 978-1-5415-7764-0
eBook ISBN: 978-1-5415-7765-7

1 –TWP–5/1/19

ELMER'S BIRTHDAY

David McKee

Andersen Press USA

Elmer, the patchwork elephant, was walking a morning walk. He said, “Good morning,” to a group of elephants and kept walking.
Once he’d gone, an elephant said, “Tomorrow is Elmer’s birthday. For a joke, let’s act as if we’ve forgotten it. Nobody wish him ‘Happy Birthday.’
At the end of the afternoon, we’ll bring out a cake and celebrate. We’ll have to warn his family and friends or it won’t work.”

"I'm not sure it's a good trick," said Bird. "But if there's cake, I'll tell the birds." The elephants chuckled and hurried off in different directions to see that nobody said "Happy Birthday."

When Lion was told, he said,
"Funny kind of joke."
Tiger said, "For Elmer's birthday? But . . ."
"Please, no buts," said the elephants. "Just do it," and they hurried off, afraid that Elmer might appear.

Cousin Wilbur was with Grandpa Eldo when they were told the plan. "You want to do that for Elmer's birthday?" said Eldo. "But . . ."

"No buts, please," said the elephant. "Just do it. Here comes Elmer, I'm off."

Elmer was nearby when the hippos and crocodiles were told.

“A trick and a cake,” said Crocodile. “Whoopee! But . . .”

“Shush!” said the elephant in a whisper. “Or Elmer will hear. And no buts, just do it.”

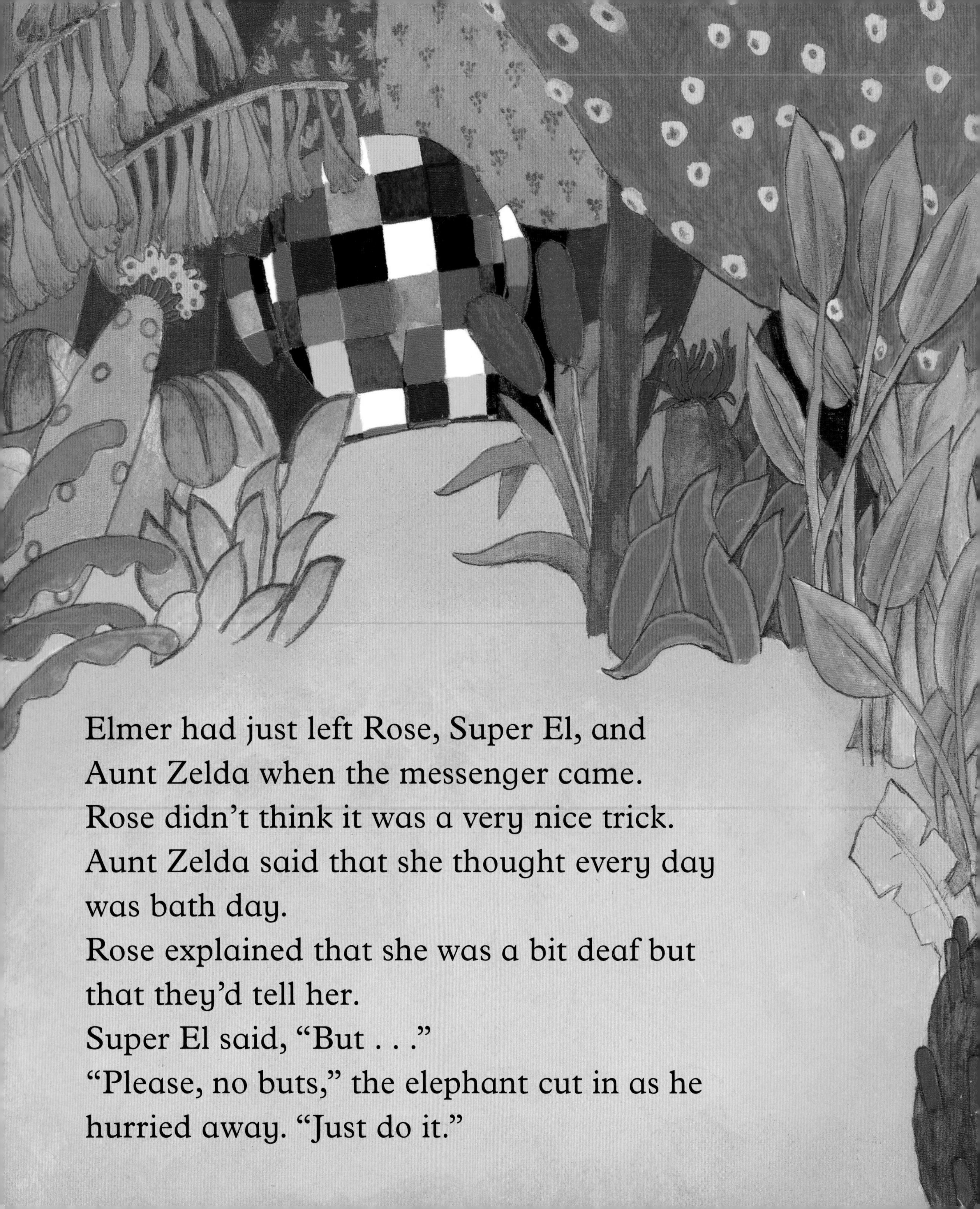

Elmer had just left Rose, Super El, and Aunt Zelda when the messenger came. Rose didn't think it was a very nice trick. Aunt Zelda said that she thought every day was bath day.
Rose explained that she was a bit deaf but that they'd tell her.
Super El said, "But . . ."
"Please, no buts," the elephant cut in as he hurried away. "Just do it."

"Any trick with cake after is a good trick," said a monkey.
"But . . ." said Giraffe.
"No buts," said an elephant. "Join in, it will be a laugh."
Snake just chuckled.

The next day, Elmer went for his usual walk.
He passed some elephants who said, "Good morning, Elmer," and then snickered.
He met Lion and Tiger, who said, "Good morning, Elmer," and didn't snicker but did seem embarrassed.
"Hmmm!" said Elmer.

He stopped and chatted with Wilbur who was just
like always.
Some birds flew by and called out, “Good morning, Wilbur.
Good MORNING, Elmer,” and flew away giggling.
“Strange,” said Elmer.
“Very,” said Wilbur.

All day similar things happened. Animals changed direction to avoid Elmer, or hurried past with a quiet "Hello."

At the end of the afternoon, Elmer suddenly found his way blocked by family and friends.
An elephant said, “Elmer, aren’t you upset? Nobody has said ‘Happy Birthday.’”
“But . . .” said Elmer, “It’s not my birthday.”
“We tried to tell them,” said Tiger, Eldo, Crocodile, Super El, and Giraffe. “But they wanted to play a joke.”
“And they promised cake,” said the monkeys.

“Cake?” said an elephant. “Cake? Whoever heard of elephants baking a cake? That’s a real joke.”
With that, the elephants brought out a huge cake.

There was silence and then they all burst out laughing. "Not bad, elephants," said Elmer. "It wasn't a brilliant trick. It isn't my birthday. But . . . the cake is a winner."